FALLEN

HAYA HUSSAIN

ISBN: 978-1-6847-0046-2 (sc)
ISBN: 978-1-6847-0045-5 (e)

Lulu Publishing Services rev. date: 07/25/2019

Notice

This book contains triggering themes, blood, and violence.
Read at your own risk.
The events, characters, and firms in this book are all fictitious.
Any similarity to actual persons, living or dead,
or to actual firms, is purely coincidental.

Foreword

Everyday,
the abyss of blue
became deeper.

It consumed
her mind,
and all she could
see,
all she could
think,
was blue.

And so,
she cut a little deeper,
thought a little shallower,
and all she could
see
was red.

1

Hello,
I am Lena Van.

Look at that,
I'm introducing myself,
like I don't know who
I am.

I mean,
I don't.

But there's nothing
wrong with that.

It's exciting
to get to know yourself
again.

See what you're
capable
of.

Re-explore.

Who knows
what you'll find
running through your veins
and thick blood?

The worst thing
you can find
is the truth,
and I think
I already found that.

Mother and Father
don't love
each other.

Frankly,
I don't love them
either.

You can't love
parents
who act like
you aren't their
child.

You can't love
parents
who don't know
how to love
each other.

You can't love
parents
that tell lies as cold as
ice.

You can't love
parents
who don't even
love each other.

2

What type of
introduction
was that?

I shared
my name
and started pitying
myself.

Let's
start over.

I am
Lena Van.

17.

Unloved.

Black-haired.

Gray-eyed.

Broken.

5'3.

Short legs.

Hurt.

Long arms.

Short torso.

Scared.

Olive skin with freckles.

Pink lips.

Lonely.

My therapist
gave me this
eyesore
of a journal.

But I guess
we share
something
in common.

We're both
eyesores.

Except I
don't have
an obnoxious
hot pink
cover.

But it's back bone is breaking,
just like me.

I, Lena Van,
step-daughter of Jason Van --
yes, *the* Jason Van
with the big company
and the alcohol issues --
have anxiety.

And the crowd
goes
wild.

At least,
Mother did.

She almost
killed herself
because her
daughter had
anxiety.

I don't blame her.

When you're
the wife
of an
almost-perfect man
and you're seeing another man
behind his back,
you would be afraid
of your daughter.

You would be afraid of what
she could say,
what
she could see,
and what
she could do.

We're very alike,
my mother
and I.

We both
have secrets,
and we both
are afraid,
but the difference is,
everybody knows my secret.

Nobody knows hers.

3

I have
to find
a place
to hide this
journal.

Sometimes,
when I'm withdrawing
the veil
and translating the
chaos
in my head,
Mother walks in.

And as soon as
I hear the
door creak,
I hide my journal
and look out the window
to see the rain
pounding on the glass.

With her
eyes narrowed,
brows furrowed,
cheeks red with
anger,
and arms crossed
as if she knows I'm
up to no-good,
she asks,

"What are you doing,
Lenithia?"

I turn my head
nonchalantly.

"Oh, just
admiring the rain,
Mother,"
I say.

She crinkles
her nose,
as if
she doesn't like the word
'mother' coming
from my filthy
mouth.

Maybe, she's afraid
that, that same mouth
will spill her
secrets.

Maybe,
she's right.

Mother says nothing,
and leaves.

She and Father
think I'm psycho.
Maybe I am.

All this
isolation
is making me
psychotic.

Father's a
coward,
afraid of what

others will
say about
me.

But not
afraid
of what I'll do
to myself,
or this family,
but to his reputation
and career.

His belt
solves all his problems
for him.

One of those problems
is me.

4

Because of all this
isolation,
I really am
going crazy.

Well, actually,
I've already
quite lost
my mind.

Writing the
insecurities
I can't think
without shuddering,
let alone speak,
in a book so a
shrink
can read
them?

Crazy.

I found
a place
to hide this.

Under a rock.

Crazy.

It's in the forest
a little past
our backyard.

All I must do
is climb over our fence,

trespass into somebody else's territory,
walk for a few minutes to the south,
and there's the big, heavy rock
where I hide
my secrets.

Absolutely.

Crazy.

I need
to get out
of this dark
room
I call my
bedroom.

But I don't want
to go
to school.

Sounds
petty.

But it isn't.

At least,
half of it
isn't.

The kids
at school
call me
a freak.

I know I am.

Must they rub
it in?

I wonder
if they'll hear
my precious
Australian accent
and stop.

Ha-ha.

There's especially
this one kid,
Kieran Ledger.

Black hair that's lighter than mine,
pretty, hazel eyes,
a jawline that could cut through glass,
thin red lips,
and a fairly muscular body,
with an addiction
to beanies.

He hates me,
but honestly,
I hate me,
too.

The bullying
started in the
9th grade.

My school
has all the grades
combined,
so it continued,
and now I'm
a senior
being bullied
by people
with

lower
calibers;
I think
highly
of myself,
don't I?

How
pathetic.

Well, Father's
home.

Did I say
"home"?

There's nothing
comforting
about this house,
except the fur carpets,
and even those are
stained
with our
white lies.

5

Lena,
you know that feeling
when you think you
know
somebody,
but then,
you realize
you really don't?

I just felt
that.

6

I have absolutely
no idea
why I am writing back.

You are a stranger
and now, you
know
my secrets.

I should be
afraid,
but I'm not.

Since you already
know so much,
it wouldn't hurt to
share some
more, right?

Yes, it would.

But I have
nothing
to lose.

Anyway,
it happened again.

The belt.

It met my back,
once again.

It lashed open
old,
almost-healed wounds.

And my mother,
she was out.

Out probably with that
married man
who has 3
children.

I wonder
if his family
is broken,
too.

It's no use
screaming
anymore.

The belt comes down
harder,
the pain doesn't
numb.

So, I simply
tremble
and let hot tears
trace their path
down my cheeks,
and onto my bloodied
clothes.

After maybe 30 minutes
of burying my head in my hands,
curled up in a corner,
wanting to not exist,
blaming myself,
I'll get up
with wobbly legs,
and search for the
bandage roll.

Which is on its
last life,
just like
me.

Sometimes,
I regret that I'm
atheist.

Not having something to
believe in
scares me.

Religion
is the only sliver of
hope
I have
left.

But imagine
how ballistic
Mother would be
if she found out
that her daughter
was trying to hang on to
something
like religion
to stay sane.

Although,
if I'm being
honest,
she's already
ballistic.

Maybe it
runs in the family.

7

Lena,
would you like to know something?

My life isn't like yours, of course.

But it has its ups and downs.

My brother's in jail for smuggling
drugs, Dad never recovered from
losing his star boy,
Ma and I are on our own.

There's security in knowing
that your dad isn't there
for sure, but knowing that he's
there, physically,
just lost in his own world, may be
one of the worst feelings ever.

Sometimes, I go over what I'll say to
my brother when I see him after
he's released.

Will he hate me for not taking care of
Dad?

Or will he be mental, too?

It eats me up inside.

I can't be Dad's star boy.

Does he see me?

When his head lolls, and his eyes dart
to every corner of that living room,
does he see me?

Or does he only see the made-up characters
in his everlasting dream?

8

I don't know
what to tell you.

I don't know
how you feel.

I don't know
what it feels to have
a father that's there,
but isn't.

I only know
how it feels to be
unloved
and alone.

But I do know how it
feels to be
fractured,
shattered,
and scared.

But I guess we're
both
scared.

Mother came home
a few hours
ago
with a beer bottle
in her hand,
threw herself onto
a couch,
and turned on one of those
rom-coms.

I wanted to tell her,

"I prefer those
old, black and white
movies,"

but then I remembered,
we aren't an
okay family.

We can't speak
to each other
unless it's to
torture the other
about their most recent
mistake.

For me,
that mistake
was being
born.

9

No reply
today?

It's a rainy day,
the journal's
damp,
but the therapist
wants this,
doesn't she?

I saw her
today.

You know what she
asked me?

"How are you?"

I didn't say anything.

If I did,
I'd only be lying to
myself.

"Are you
okay?"
she asked.

I nodded.

"Can I read your
journal?"

I answered with
silence.

"Lenithia,
this will be no use
if you continue
to bottle up
everything."

Again,
silence.

So,
she sighed,
scribbled something
down,
glanced at me,
and went through
the routine.

"So, what did you do
this week?"

My eyes stayed
on the black rug.

"Watched the rain,
read a book,
and wrote in the journal."

My voice
is very silent.

My Australian accent
is the only thing
that people can
understand about me.

She nodded,
scribbled some more,
glanced at me
like I was a

guinea pig,
and continued to
write more things down.

"Have you started
school
yet?"

I wanted to answer:
*I'm already going through
one hell,
I don't need
to go through
another.*

But I just
shook my head,
and once again,
the soft scratch of her pencil
against the yellow
notepad
filled the silence.

And we continued
with her scribbling
and me telling lies.

10

Lena,
your full name is beautiful.

Lenithia.

It sounds pleasant.

11

No story today,
Mr./Ms. Stranger?

What a
pity.

A little bit of
something to read,
someone to think about
besides me,
or Mother,
or Father
would make these
long days
a bit more
enticing.

That sounds
insensitive,
doesn't it?

Well, thank
you.

But I'm pretty sure
one of my nurses
named me,
since Mother
was cursing
my existence.

I wonder
what stopped
her
from getting an
abortion,

because it wasn't
me.

It's 3 AM
right now.

I'll have to sneak out
tomorrow,
to put the
journal
away.

If you're wondering
why I'm up so late,
it's because Father came home
2 hours ago,
took out the broom
and hit my legs,

They're quite red.

He's never done it on my
legs.

It stings,
and I can tell
that'll I'll be
sore
tomorrow.

So, right now,
I'm sitting with ice pressed to my legs,
hissing
when I press too hard.

I just need
something,
maybe even
someone,
to get me out of here.

Something to
run away.

Far,
far,
so far
away.

12

Lena,
get better
soon.

Please.

You asked for a
story,
right?

Well, here's one.

In freshmen year,
I saw this girl
in my art class.

She drew this
lovely
portrait
of someone,
and I didn't know
who it was,
but when I asked,
she looked at me,
glanced back at her
masterpiece,
and cocked her head to the side.

She granted me
nothing but a sad glint in
her eyes,
and still,
to this day,
3 years later,

I wonder
who that
beautiful woman
she drew
was.

13

Intriguing story,
really.

Who was
the girl
that was
painting,
if you don't mind
me asking?

Did her eyes
look broken,
as if she couldn't
hold the burden of
living?

Did her eyes
hold the burdens
her shoulders
could not bear?

Well, I hope
I get to
meet her
someday, because
we might just
have something
in common.

14

If you were
wondering
where the journal was
last night,
or whenever you take it
from under that
rock,
it was because
I wasn't ready for a
reply.

I don't know
why.

Anyways,
I kind of want to
go back
to school.

I miss this
guy,
or rather,
I miss his
face.

His name
is Parker,
blond hair,
blue eyes,
the bulkiest
body,
and high cheekbones.

Did I mention the
eyelashes?

When it snows,
sometimes
the snowflakes
fall on them,
and I could
stare
forever.

But he
would never
see me.

Not when
he has a
girlfriend
who's more concerned about her
unnatural
body parts,
eyelashes,
and eyebrows
than what her boyfriend's
saying about her
when she doesn't have him
on a leash.

I've liked
him
since the 9th grade,
but
he has no idea
who I am.

All I know
is that he's an
okay

guy
with a
stunning
face.

I think
I'm too afraid
to know
anything else.

15

Lena,
I saw your father
and your mother
enrolling you
in school.

But I didn't
see you.

16

I prefer
to stray
from places
where my parents
are.

Especially
when they're
together.

So, I simply
said I didn't want to go,
even though that
jostled up
father's gears.

And, dear stranger,
you just revealed
that you go
to my school.

Quite careless.

Not
that I'm
calling you out
on a mistake.

Just
something I
noticed.

Speaking of
which,
I notice
a lot
of things.

And I sometimes
wish
I could
shut down
my
eyes
and brain
so I won't
think
too much.

Because then I start
seeing
blue.

But I found
an
escape.

A
paperclip
from Father's
desk.

I think it's called
'cutting'?

Yes, *that*.

It's
relieving,
for a while.

But then all the
emotions
come back,
and once
again,
I start

seeing
blue.

But in that
small
snippet of
time,
I see
red.

Red.

Like the
sprout
of droplets,
coming from the
vein
on my
wrist,
I see
red.

Red.

And for a moment,
amongst the
pain
and the sting,
I forget
everything
and I let
bliss
overtake
my mind.

And I
love
it.

17

Lena,
you can't
do this
to yourself.

Stop,
please.

It's wrong,
and you know it.

So, please,
stop.

Stop blaming
yourself
and punishing
your body
for what you can't
control.

18

If it's so
wrong,
why does it
feel
so
right?

19

You didn't
answer,
maybe because
you didn't know what to
say.

Well,
anyways,
I went to the
shrink
again,
and we went through
the same
routine.

"How are you
today,
Lenithia?"

No answer.

She scribbled
something,
then glared at me
with her
cold
blue eyes.

"What have you
written
in your
journal
so far?"

she asked,
as if expecting
me to answer.

But everybody
expects
something.

I've learned if you
don't have any
expectations,
then you won't be
disappointed.

"Nothing,"

I lie.

She nods,
scribbling
something down.

I realize now
as I'm retelling
today's events
that
the shrink
will never be able to
help
me because
I keep
lying.

So,
once again,
I am wasting
my parents'
money.

I guess
I should be
grateful
that they are
willing
to help me find
asylum.

Even
if it means
I must
wake up
with sore
limbs
and scabs.

Living under a
roof
is better than
living on the
streets.

So,
I should be
grateful.

Then why
do I not
feel grateful?

Whatever.

I'm beginning
to think
too much
again.

So, I take
the paperclip,
slide it under my skin,
edging it
into my flesh,
and letting it prick a
vein.

It's
happening
again.

20

Lena,
you need to
stop
punishing yourself.

I'm saying this again
because I know
that you're hurting,
and I know what's
causing the hurt.

It's not your
fault,
Lenithia.

So, stop
blaming
yourself.

You're only making it worse
for yourself.

Don't.

Let yourself
breathe.

You're bottling
your
emotions up,
so I suggest
you talk to the
therapist.

Just not about
me.

21

I don't want to come off as
rude
or
conceited,
but I don't need
another
therapist.

Maybe,
I will
talk to the shrink,
but when I'm
ready.

Right now,
I'm just
doubting everything.

I'm doubting
this journal.

I'm doubting
myself.

My wants.

My needs.

My despair.

I'm losing
hope.

I went to school yesterday.

Saw Parker's face,
and I think
I'm in love.

With a
jerk,
of course,
but I think
he's my
first love.

And then his
girlfriend
came up to him
and sucked his face off.

Ew.

She wears clothes
that I'm sure
cost more than a few
bucks.

Designer bags,
gets her nails done
twice a week,
has a stylist,
owns two phones;
one for texting,
the other for taking
pictures.

Sometimes, I gag
at how spoiled some
people
can be.

Kieran Ledger
came up to me.

Snatched a drawing
I was working on.

He's very tall.

6'0.

I'm 5'3.

I couldn't reach it.

I didn't say anything,
I kept quiet
because I don't
want
to become
vulnerable.

I never
got it back.

I hate him.

No, wait.

I strongly
dislike
him.

It's hard for me to
hate someone.

Because then
I start being
grateful.

So, what am I
grateful
to him for?

For being
obsessed
with my drawings?

At least,
he makes my art
feel wanted.

I went home
and after Father
took out his
fury,
I cried into my
pillow.

I told myself I was strong
because I had made it
through another day
without running
away.

But if I were
strong,
then this torture
wouldn't have occurred,
would it?

None of these
panic
attacks,
or doubts,
or pain,
or pain*killers*.

Pain*killers* help
pain,
they really do.

They numb
me
and they drain
me of power.

Make me
forget.

But then
I realize
that
numb is worse
than pain.

Numb is that
tingling feeling
when you realize
there is no
hope.

Hope is that
stunning feeling
when you realize
there's still a
chance.

A chance is
what I don't
have.

22

Lena,
do you know what
hope is?

Besides something you
need,
something you
crave,
something you
want,
something you
envy?

It stands for these four words:
Hang On, Pain Ends.

It does,
doesn't it?

But it gets
trapped
in a lonely corner,
and it haunts you.

It leaves a lashed
mark
that only you can see.

Those girls who love their boyfriends,
those boys who hold their girlfriends,
those teachers who fell in love with teaching,
those parents who met love and did something with it,
they do not see what you see.

They do not see the difficulty that has encased you.

Is that their fault?

Are they supposed to reach into your heart
and see how many years of
pain have been circulating in your
blood flow?

Or is it your fault?

Are you supposed to talk to them
and show your pain
and confide in them about your
tangled life
and your mother's affair?

Or is it nobody's fault?

Are we all going through pain
but in different variations
and should we all know the
level of pain in another's body,
just like we all look at the moon,
all for a different reason?

Or is it just you in this dark,
isolated,
cruel world?

23

I realize
how right you are.

But if I never
smile,
how come
nobody *ever*
notices?

Hah, that's
unreasonable.

But to be fair,
you wouldn't have noticed
if it weren't for my
writing.

Sometimes,
I wonder
if you're an illusion.

Sometimes,
I wonder
if I'm making
all of this up.

I feel like I want to
jump.

Just jump off the
balcony
and *fall*.

And then I want to
keep
falling.

And now I'm deadpanning
that, that'll hurt.

So,
I must go through
pain
to end my
pain?

Why must everything be so
malicious?

I don't
want
to feel pain.

But I'd rather
feel pain
than nothing.

I like the way
my heart
skips
when Parker
walks by.

But I hate the way
when he stares
into his
brunette girlfriend's
beautiful
green eyes.

I tell myself
it isn't real.

And I can believe it,
if I say it out
loud.

Everything becomes
more believable
once you say it loud enough
for everyone to hear.

I noticed something
again.

I'm easy
to manipulate.

Paperclip.

I need to find
a better blade.

24

Lena,
sometimes it's better
to be manipulated
than to manipulate.

25

They know.

The girls,
the boys,
the teachers,
they *know*.

My secret is out.

It was already out,
but it was just
Mother,
Father,
and the therapist
at first.

And
you.

But they
all
know.

And they whisper.

They snicker.

They laugh.

They point.

And I know
that it's not
Father,
because his reputation
is at stake.

Maybe
Mother.

Not the
therapist
because she'd
lose her job.

Maybe
you.

So,
I'm not placing the journal
under the
rock.

I'm sorry,
but I don't
trust you.

At least,
not for
now.

What I'm most afraid of
is Father.

I can imagine
how furious
he will be when he
comes home.

I don't think I can handle any pain
after what **Kieran** Ledger
and his friend did to
me.

I was walking
to my next class

and they pulled me into one
of the closets
and kicked me
just below the ribs,
and slightly in the hips,
along with a punch
to the eye
and a slit from the girl's
long nails
on my collarbone.

The bell rang,
making me late.

They ran off,
Kieran leaving his
black beanie.

Somehow,
he still has a
handsome
face
and I don't
hate
him.

So, I went to
the bathroom,
washed my face,
opened lockers without locks
until I found makeup
and covered the blackeye and placed
a Band-Aid I got from the nurse
on the slit on my collarbone.

Then I
pretended
like my ribs

weren't about to
explode
and that I could
actually walk
without my hips hurting
and my eye
welling with tears.

I
cried
when I got
home.

I
sobbed,
and it wasn't
pretty.

And
Mother
was out
and Father
was at
work.

So, I let the words
flow out in my tears,
because I know I could
never say them.

And I finally
accepted
that I was
broken.

And it hurt
so
much.

I'm broken.

Do you hear that?

I'm broken.

I'll say it again,
I'm
broken.

B-R-O-K-E-N.

Is this what **Kieran** Ledger wanted?

Is this what Mother wanted?

Is this what Father wanted?

I'm broken,
okay?

I'm finally
broken.

26

Father
came 'home'.

He was
drunk,
probably drinking
because everybody
at work
had something
to
say.

He knocked on
my door,
which was locked,
and said,

"Lenithia,
sweetheart,
open up,"

like he actually
cared
about what I was
doing.

I started
sobbing
harder.

I was so
scared.

I was
trembling.

For the first time
in so long,
I was scared
of how hard the
belt
would come down,
if it was even going to be
the belt.

I shook
uncontrollably,
and the hot tears
kept coming
endlessly.

My body
was already sore
from the first
punishment I had gotten
for being who
I was.

The knocks came
harder,
like hail,
and his slurred voice became
louder.

"Open up!
Open up or I'll break
the door!"

And I blurred everything
he said afterwards
out of my mind.

All I remember
is that he *did*
break down the door,

a black
belt
in one hand
and a bottle in the other,
and that I started sobbing
even louder.

I also remember
that Mother was
standing outside
doing nothing
to stop it.

Just watching,
as if
I deserved it.

I tried moving to the corner,
but I just trapped myself.

I remember him
screaming at me,
telling me my worth,
telling me how *useless* I was,
how ever since I had been born
I had done *nothing* good
to this family.

How my existence was a mistake,
how I had ruined everything,
how I had ruined my mother's life
along with his.

How everything about me
was disgusting,
how my face was a disgrace,
how *I* was a disgrace.

It was funny,
really,
because he was only
there
for my mother.

And she didn't love him.

So, I feel bad for him.

But I'm still grateful,
even as I'm in bed,
with my door locked,
hiding in my bedsheets,
trying to get away
from everything,
that he provided me with
schooling
and a
place to live.

Because he's the one getting
cheated.

I'm not being
lied to.

I'm just getting the
brutal
truth.

He's the one
who married a woman
who doesn't love him,
who has a daughter from another man,
who is seeing another man,
and can't even look at his face.

He's the one
who's housing a girl
who does nothing but disappoint,
who can't do anything right,
who is useless,
and can't even love herself.

So, I guess
I'm grateful.

Even though
the bandage roll is finished,
my hip is hurting,
my black eye is getting worse,
my lip is swollen,
my rib cage is throbbing,
my back is aching,
and my legs are tinted red from blood.

Yet,
I'm still grateful.

27

I didn't go to
school
today.

I figured
nobody would miss me,
and that Father
wouldn't have to hear
from anyone.

It might quench
Father's thirst.

Mother was out the whole day,
probably fixing a family
that isn't hers,
leaving her own
to be broken.

Right now,
it's raining
again.

I like it
when it rains.

It's very
peaceful.

Sometimes,
I like to watch
the raindrops
hit my window pane
and listen to the harmony.

I don't listen
to a lot of music,
partly because I don't have anything
to play music with,
and because I have never
been exposed
to music.

Except of course when those bands
One Direction
or
BTS
release a song
and the girls
won't stop talking about it.

Once again,
I notice
too much.

Is that possible?

Noticing too much?

Who knows.

Anyways,
I'm feeling particularly
grateful
today.

There isn't any sunshine
so I don't have to
match moods with the day
and act like everything's okay.

There are no stares
because I haven't stepped out of
the house.

There is only silence,
the rustle of my black bedsheets and white
fur pillows
as I move about,
and the scratch of the pencil
against this journal's
paper.

There's also the security
that someone out there
is going through something worse
than what I am going through,
so it's okay.

I don't have the right
to be
ungrateful.

I'm sure whichever force
that created me
and the world around us
has a plan for me.

It doesn't have to be good
and it doesn't have to be bad,
it just has to be a plan.

A *purpose.*

A *reason.*

A *will.*

Something along
those lines.

It's 11:18 AM.

A Friday.

At school,
they would probably
be having lunch.

Parker's girlfriend
sitting in his lap,
feeding him those potato
chips
and smacking her lips
on his cheek and
walking off in those
branded shoes
like she owns the place.

Ew.

One of the reasons
Parker will never
notice me
is that I never
wear anything
above my ankles.

Nobody
can ever see my
legs
or my
arms.

I like it
that way.
The less you expose,
the less
others can judge
you on.

And I know
that beauty
nowadays

is nudity and skin,
but it doesn't bother me
that much.

Mostly because
I've never felt
comfortable in my own skin,
so how could I wear it proudly?

Maybe I should
drop out.

Father would be
furious.

All these years
worth of textbooks,
supplies,
only to drop out?

He would
disown
me.

Mother wouldn't stop him.

Besides,
senior year will end,
and I will have to find
a college.

Most likely a
run-down,
never-heard-of
college.

Father would never
be willing to pay for a school like
Silver Creek Academy.

Silver Creek Academy
is the best university
in our state.

It's an art university,
so Father wouldn't even
let me speak
about it.

He thinks
art
is going to get me
nowhere.

You know,
it's funny
how I call him
Father.

We are not
biologically
related,
and he doesn't
love me further
than the extent of
getting me a nice bed
next to a window
with some pretty pillows
and a roof to live under.

Still,
I am
grateful.

28

It's finally
the weekend.

Father came home yesterday,
but strangely,
he didn't do
or even say
anything.

Another reason
to be
grateful.

My body
has more time
to heal.

My legs
are drawn
to my chest,
a black blanket covering my
broken body.

I don't know
what the world
has in store
for me.

I'm beginning
to think
too much
again.

I get up,
my wrist yearning
for the paper clip.

My body
and my mind
yearning for
the bliss
that comes
when the little
droplets
of blood
sprout
from my
veins.

It sounds
sick,
it really does,
but it's what I
think.

It's what goes on in my
head.

I can't
control it.

The thoughts
come and
they go,
and if I'm lucky enough
(like right now)
I can catch them and
write them down as a
chapter
in my life.

There are
shadows
in my life
that become

darker
than inky
black,
and maybe I should
illuminate
them.

Add some
light.

But you can't have
light
without the
dark,
right?

You need to know
what the night is
to see the sun.

If there were no
sunset,
no
midnight,
could you
appreciate
the day?

There would be no
sunrise,
no
new tide.

I pick up the
shining
paperclip
and look at it,
interrogating it,
trying to

understand it.

I'm psycho.

I've lost my mind.

Trying to
understand
an inanimate
object?

Crazy.

I smile
softly to myself,
laughing
at how
ridiculous
I am.

Maybe I'll speak
to the therapist
on Monday.

Actually speak.

Not just incomplete
phrases,
but real
phrases
with meaning
and genuine
morals.

Maybe even
questions.

I've never been
allowed to ask those.

I have always been
told.

What to do,
what to wear,
what to eat.

I've never answered,
either.

Once again,
I have always been told.

Never asked.

No options,
no exceptions,
no privileges.

You do it,
or you leave.

Or you get dealt with.

As I move to
sit back down
on my bed,
my body stretches.

The scabs from
previous beatings
stretch and crack,
and I can feel
warm blood
seeping through,
staining my
clothes.

I take the
front
of my hand
and lay it down
on my thigh,
my eyes
glaring at the
one vein
branching from my wrist
and moving
upward through my hand.

I take the
paperclip
with my left hand
and slide it under the skin,
a new kind of pain
overcoming
my mind.

Pain distracts me
from reality.

Turning my back
to the world,
blinding my eyes to the reality,
it helps.

It's like being drunk;
you forget everything,
become careless for
a while,
then wake up
and everything
comes back at you.

It never really goes away.

That's why it's toxic.

*You aren't sober
when you
cut.*

You zone out
into
your own world,
oblivious of
reality.

There are no restraints,
you aren't sober.

It feels so
good
to be lost
for once.

I guess that's why lost people
drink.

To get lost
all over again.

The first moments
you get lost,
you don't realize it.

For the first few seconds,
everything seems
perfectly okay,
like a blank canvas.

Then, it comes to you,
like a tidal wave
in Malibu,
getting bigger by the moment.

It hits,
and you go under
into the
deep blue,
surrounded by
blue.

Everything is just
blue.

You can't reach the
top,
your lungs are failing,
your body is becoming tired,
your mind foggy,
and there's one
thought
echoing in that
hollow mind of yours.

So yes, I'm
lost.

And then it
begins.

You sink,
deeper
and
deeper
and
deeper
and
deeper.

Then you think:
why were you treading
such dangerous
waters anyways?

There's a reason
when you go to the beach and
the water calls your name.

Sometimes,
the water taunts you.

Sometimes,
the water knows you'll come on your own.

That's why beaches are
alluring.

There's a beach for
everyone.

One that
summons them,
ready to drag them
under.

Everybody starts
somewhere.

I've been treading
dangerous waters
for a long time now.

It's hard to admit it,
but red
is temporary.

Blue
is forever.

29

I placed
the journal
under the rock
last night.

I didn't get a reply.

I'm beginning to
doubt
again.

I'm
sorry
for not
trusting you.

If that's what
I did wrong.

Before I go back to
school,
I need someone
to talk to.

I don't even
know who you are,
but I still
need you.

Your words
matter.

But now,
I wonder,
if I was living
in a dream,

and I have finally
woken up.

Living in a dream
where I wanted
someone to be
there.

But if it were
a dream,
then the old entries
wouldn't still
be in the journal.

I am all over the place.

I am worn down.

My body is aching.

Painkillers it is,
then.

30

Nobody loves you.

31

Please,
tell me
something new.

I'm aware.

Why must you
remind
me?

What happened to all
the kind
and subtle
messages?

I'm leaving
for school,
and I want you to know
I woke up to
this.

32

Your face is a disgrace.

33

I'm not putting the
journal
under the rock
tonight.

I know I asked for
too much
when I said
I dreamt of a shoulder
to cry on,
but I was hoping desperately
that it would happen.

I guess
I was
being hopeful.

And now
doubt is piling over me
like
rolling
waves.

The worst part is
the waves
are
blue.

I'm drowning
in blue.

And I'm sinking deeper
and deeper
and deeper.

I want to
reach
red.

I need
red.

I just
crave
the bliss
of
red.

The color that blinds
my eyes,
hypnotizes
my brain,
blurs out
my thoughts.

Red.

Redder
than a blooming
rose.

Redder
than the blood
in my veins.

And I'm so,
so,
so
stubborn.

More stubborn
than gray,

which refuses to leave
and causes static
in my mind.

Gray
is when I'm
confused.

Like
I'm buffering.

Like
I'm loading
and thinking.

Gray is
stubborn,
and so am I,
because I'm not listening to
my brain
when it says
not to put the journal
under
the rock.

34

Nobody wants to see you breathing.

35

You are worthless.

36

I am tired.

I am tired
of the bullying,
of the punching,
of the kicking,
of the glares,
of the hitting,
of the yelling,
of the scolding.

And I am tired
of being
tired.

So tired.

I am
so, *so*
tired
of being
tired.

And yet,
I keep placing
this journal
under the rock.

The lake
a few yards
past the woods
is calling my name.

No,
it is *screaming*
it.

It is *screaming* my name.

My
name.

Only
my
name.

And I will obey.

I will obey.

37

Get rid of yourself.

38

Do the world a favor and die.

39

You don't belong in this world.

40

Nobody can look at me
anymore.

Not after my attempt.

I let my fingers
graze the clear ice
of the lake
with my hand,
and *nobody said anything.*

The neighbors
who retreated to their
homes
as they saw me
said *nothing.*

I brought down
the hammer
in my hand
against the ice,
and when the ice broke away,
I
jumped.

Nothing happened.

No one came out of their
houses,
they simply watched
from their windows,
some recording it.

They didn't do *anything.*

I can't help
but resent them
for that.

They just had to *do*
something,
even if it was to
take a block of ice
and block
the only opening.

I let my body sink,
the water fill my lungs,
and the cold, prickling water tear my consciousness
away,
but then a hand came
and pulled me out.

I couldn't see
who it was,
partly because my eyes
were fuzzy
and I was lightheaded.

I just know
that their lips met mine,
and I could breathe again.

After a spurt of water erupted from
my lungs.

I remember
them picking me up
and laying me on the porch
of the house.

In that moment,
as I laid on my side,
my eyes trying to gain focus

and my mind trying to stay conscious,
I had so many people to blame.

But I didn't
want
to blame them.

There was **Kieran**.

There was Mother.

There was Father.

I'm going to place
this journal
where it always goes.

I'll find a way.

I always do.

Now I'm locked up
in my room
because my father
is afraid
that I'll attempt suicide again
and damage his reputation.

He's right.

I would do it all over again,
and this time, I'd do it
right.

41

You should be dead.

42

You are not
the person
who was replying to me
earlier.

Or are you bipolar?

Or are you **Kieran**?

In fact, were you **Kieran**
this whole entire time?

Was this some kind of
cruel
joke
where you made me feel wanted,
then told everybody,
beat me up
to make sure that I knew
I was inferior,
left a scar on my collarbone
to leave an imprint,
and started leaving hateful
messages to
laugh
at me?

I still want to know
what you'll say,
though.

But
I don't want to know
who you
are.

Don't tell me
who you
are,
because I
fear
the answer.

43

Lena Van,
I was flipping through the old entries.

I can assure you that, that wasn't me.

I care for you,
Lena Van.

I have *always* cared for you,
and didn't you notice how I always address
my entry, and that person didn't?

Even if you don't want to know who I am,
I am someone beyond your limitation.

I am someone who you would
least expect to be answering you.

I hope you feel better, Lena,
even though that may be too much
to ask for.

44

I went to school,
and Parker talked to me.

Oh gosh, he talked to me.

And, oh gosh,
I screwed up.

Oh gosh,
I screwed up
so bad.

He said,
"hello, Lena"

and I just
mumbled.

And then,
he asked me how
I was,
and I just *stared.*

I
stared.

And I know
he doesn't
care,
because he smiled
(forcefully)
and left.

He didn't say goodbye,
and I was glad he didn't,
but at the same time,

I wasn't.

I wasn't at *all.*

Not at all.

And now I am fighting
my two partitions:
the wiser me,
and the pathetic me.

45

Lena Van,
stay away from him.

There's something wrong,
and I know it.

46

How do
you
know?

47

Lena Van,
you shouldn't question it.

I just know.

48

You seem
to know
a lot of things.

Most of them being
things
you shouldn't.

And
didn't I tell you
I was stubborn?

Maybe not with people,
but with
talking diaries?

Yes.

Anyways,
I have butterflies
in my stomach.

Parker's here,
he's in my room.

He's working on our assigned project,
and his hair
is falling into his eyes
so perfectly.

And his blue eyes;
they are shining
with such
entity.

He looked up.

Just now,
he looked up,
and gave me that
warm smile
of his.

He has no idea
how
he makes me
feel.

And I know
it is stupid to tell you this,
but I can't help it.

There's nothing holding
me back.

Right now,
in this room,
with Parker,
I feel like a bird
that was let out
of its cage.

You know,
I've realized something.

I don't
write
in this journal
for myself anymore.

Well, maybe
a little bit,
but mostly
so I can tell *you*
things.

49

Lena Van,
trust me when I say you should stay away from him.

He was the one who wrote those horrible entries.

I hate to say this,
but you're gullible and easy to manipulate,
Lenithia.

I don't know how he got his hands on that journal,
but he did.

So, stay away from him.

50

I believe
you.

For whatever
reason,
I believe you.

And I don't want to,
but I must.

I could
hate
you
for telling me the
truth,
but that wouldn't be
fair.

But if I don't
hate
you,
then I'll
start
hating
myself
for liking
a guy
like
Parker.

Actually,
I
hate
myself
already,
so that's fine.

To be fair,
though,
I don't know
for certain
if you're telling the truth.

But you're right about one thing:
I *am* gullible.

51

Lena Van,
I've always wanted to be the one
person that you could count on.

The one person that didn't try
to deceive you.

I'm sorry, for everything.

It's funny,
how I wanted to be your knight
in shining armor, yet I hurt you
anyways.

52

I don't
know
what to say.

I don't
know
who you are.

What am I
supposed to say
to someone who claims
they know me?

And in
reality,
I guess
you really do,
don't you?

When you walk
by me,
do you realize
how
vulnerable
I am around you?

Do you realize
that I
am always cowering
in fear,
afraid that
someone around me
knows my weaknesses?

You
are my
Achille's Heel.

53

Lena Van,
I wouldn't hurt you.

I may be a horrible person, and
I might not be dependable, but
I would never in a million years
hurt you.

I wouldn't use all of this
to my advantage.

What would I get, Lenithia?

Would I get satisfaction from
stomping on a fragile and broken
girl?

You're broken, Lena, and I
see it. I see it when you walk
down the school halls. I see it
in the way you write. *I see it,*
and I swear to God I blame myself
for how broken you are.

I'm a horrible person, Lena.

I truly am.

But I would never hurt you
to the extent that you could never
look in the mirror to check your
reflection.

I've hurt you before, I must admit.

I didn't mean it. Any of it. I'll say
it again, and again, and again,
just to make sure that you know
to stay away from me, which isn't
really fair of me to say since I won't
let you leave me.

I'm stubborn.

And I'm sorry.

But sorry isn't enough to make up
for what I've done to you.

54

I can't say
it's okay,

But I can say that I'll forget
what you did,
and what you said.

Maybe not
how you made me
feel,
but I don't know who
you are,
so I don't know
how bad
of a person
you are.

Sometimes,
I stay up late
thinking about
who you are.

I've come up with some pretty
crazy
ideas.

Like
Dad.

He's done a lot,
but he doesn't go to school
with me,
obviously.

Maybe
Parker.

I know he was you
at one point.

But it's unlikely.

Maybe
Kieran.

To be fair,
everybody's done
a lot.

The craziest
idea
is Mother.

She'd kill herself
rather than even
try
to talk to me.

55

It's turning upside down.

Everything.

My world,
my whole world.

I found
Mother
in the bathtub
today
after I came home.

Not her,
her *body*.

I can't stop
crying.

I saw her,
a gun clutched in her hand,
blood coloring the water
a bloody pink,
and blood running down her forehead.

I screamed.

I screamed louder than I had ever screamed before.

Louder
than when Father uses
two belts.

Louder
than when I have
those nightmares.

I screamed
at the world,
wanting to know
what I did wrong.

Wanting to know
why *I* had to be
the first one
to see the gore.

I screamed
at the power
that made me,
wanting to know
why I was
me.

Wanting to know
why I was such a burden
and nuisance to my mother
that she just couldn't take it
anymore.

I collapsed,
my knees quivering,
not being able to move,
just watching the water
rushing from the pipe,
almost overflowing,
dyed red.

Not being able to get up
and do something.

Why didn't I do something?

Why didn't I call the police?

Or check her pulse?

What if she had been faintly breathing,
and I could've saved her?

What if I could've saved her,
but she died because I had a panic attack,
and shunned everything out?

I could've done something,
anything,
anything,
but I just stood there,
falling to the tiled floor and
sobbing as my body
shook violently.

Coward.

You *sick,*
horrible,
useless,
coward.

56

Lena Van,
I know you're not okay,
so it's pointless to ask.

You didn't come to school
today, either. News spread
quick. Everybody knows.

I'm not good at comforting
people, to be honest. But
everything will be fine,
Lenithia. I'll try my best
to hush everybody. Nobody
blames you.

You're not the criminal here,
Lena. You're not the one to blame.

You found her, and that's what
matters.

If she had been alive, Lena,
you would have been the last
person she would have seen.

Be grateful.

Sometimes, it's okay to not be
the hero.

57

You were wrong.

You said
nobody
would blame me.

Everybody
thinks it's my
fault.

That *I'm*
the freak.

That either
I killed my own
mother,
or I was the reason
she killed herself.

I was probably the
reason
she killed herself.

I want to be okay
with that,
act like it's something
I get all the time,
but it's *not*.

Because it's the first time
that someone has
actually
died because of me.

This is real.

This isn't some nightmare
I hoped I could
wake up from.

It's real.

I can't scream
in the middle of the night,
nightgown soaked in sweat
and wake up and tell myself
"it's not real, it's not real"
and simply go back to sleep.

No, it's not like that.

Now, I have to
face
and embrace
the horror
that someone actually
took their own life
because I was
a burden.

The police searched our house,
tried to find
a
suicide note.

They left without one.

I still looked for one,
even in that secret compartment
in Mother's closet.

Nothing.

There was *nothing*.

No goodbye.

She left, and she left
without a will,
without a last word
to her daughter.

When was the last time we
spoke?

What had she said?

I can't remember.

I can't remember.

I can't remember the last words
my mother said to me.

I can't remember.

58

Lena Van,
It's okay.

You and your mother barely ever
talked. And that isn't your fault.
You could've been a better daughter,
and she could've been a much better
mother.

You tried your best, Lenithia. You
tried, and you tried, and you kept
trying. But it didn't work. Your
mother didn't realize it.

It's not your fault, so stop blaming
yourself.

You don't deserve this, any of this.

You deserve better, Lena. Much better.

59

Please,
just tell me who you are.

Please, I must
know.

I can't stand
secrets any
longer.

Not knowing
has become my greatest
fear.

I'm afraid I'll be
stuck in my own world
like *that* day,
just watching the moment
pass by,
my head in havoc
and my heart pounding fast.

My life
isn't
a video game.

I don't have three lives.

I don't have three chances.

This is it.

I only have one life,
and one chance.

I don't want to be in
oblivion
the whole time.

Please, just tell me.

I'll take it.

I'll do whatever I have to,

60

Lena Van,
I knew this day would come sooner or later.
One day, at one time, I'd have to tell you
who I was.

This is it, isn't it?

After this you'll see me in a different way,
you'll spend hours looking at that scar on your
collar bone in the mirror.

Maybe when you see me in the hallways,
you'll think of me differently. Whether that
be good or bad, I don't know.

I know you don't like me.

You might think this is a twisted game after this.

I'm sorry, for breaking your trust and ruining
everything.

You're right. Life isn't a video game.

You only have one life, one chance. I'm risking
a lot right now, Lena.

You probably don't trust me, how could you? I'm
a bully, a literal *bully*.

And I found this journal in the woods behind my
house, hidden under a big rock. The cover, I must
admit, threw me off. Surely Lena Van, the girl in all
black wouldn't own a hot pink journal, right?

I took it with me, which I admit, was wrong. It was
basically stealing. But then I read your entries. I was
drawn in by your words, Lenithia. Every single one of
them.

The way your y's curved and the way your a's were rounded,
I was drawn, reeled in, and your writing was my bait.

I fell deep into this abyss, and I decided to write you back.

Maybe, it wasn't a good idea, but we're here now right?

It's crazy. I never meant for this to happen.

When I read your name, when I figured out
who you were, my nose didn't scrunch in distaste. I
smiled.

I don't hate you, Lenithia Emma-Rose Van. I never have,
and I never will. I may have hurt you countless of times before,
but I would never in a million years ever try to break you.

I know you think that, but it's not true. I admire you. I've
always admired you. From the very beginning when I saw you
walk in with your hair in a ponytail and
that white sweatshirt and
black leggings.

Those gray eyes met mine and time stopped for a minute. I
thought you were cold, emotionless.

Like a machine, programmed for a certain
reason and only one reason.

I thought that was it, there was nothing more to you.

Then I got to know you. You were an artist and liked to
draw. You were pretty good at it, too. You were the girl

who drew that portrait I told you about.

I think I finally figured it out, Lena. You drew the person
you *wanted* to be. I called her pretty, didn't
I? But I didn't call *you* pretty.

It was the first time I saw despair flicker in your eyes.

You barely ever spoke. You were a quiet person.

I liked that about you. You observed more and talked less.
You had a keen eye, too. Sometimes the teachers would ask
you to pick colors for their own paintings.

You'd just point.

I thought you were mute.

Until I heard you speak in that sweet Australian accent.

I never expected it; I had no idea you were an Aussie.

You surprised me.

You always do.

I think I'll surprise you, too, now.

I'm Kieran, Kieran Ledger. The same boy
that made your life living hell in the hallways.

The same one that kicked you and hurt you.

When I said I was a horrible person, I meant
it.

I'm a horrible person. A horrible person that
found someone like you.

Author's Note

Fallen is a work that I archived for a year, and to be honest, the first version was very rusty, and I had been making it up as I went. I have a bad habit of not plotting out my books. This is the re-written version, a new and improved copy.

I changed many aspects, for example, it would be **Kieran's** sister who would be an outlaw, and she wouldn't have been their father's star child. She would have been a goth, and out of jealousy, she was to kill their parents, be arrested, leaving **Kieran** on his own.

At first, my initial idea was for the person who was writing Lena back to be Parker, but that would have been too predictable and a foreseen cliché.

Lena's story is purely fictional; I have never met someone or been through anything like this. I chose a sensitive topic to write about because people are sitting in their homes, blind to what impact their words may leave on someone, even if it is the demeanor they say 'hello' in. Reality is much more cruel than warm bedsheets and romcoms.

The reason colors are used to describe Lena's experience is because these feelings are indescribable. Words are not enough to describe most things. "Indescribable" is broad and shallow. There's so much more to what people feel. We can't come up with new words, but they say that a picture is worth thousands of words.

A picture is a frozen moment, captured in time and permanently put into a small frame. A picture can be a painting. Instead of using pictures to indicate the emotional toll that Lena experienced, I decided to use colors. Each color is linked to an inanimate object in real life.

Gray is the paper clip. The paper clip is stubborn, because its owner doesn't listen to her crying body and others who care about her. Red is blood, because Lena finds bliss from cutting herself. It's not that she's a psychopath; she doesn't find bliss in piercing her skin or watching the blood rise. She finds bliss in knowing that she's escaping reality. The pain distracts her, and all Lenithia wants is a distraction. Blue is the ocean. When we were learning a song, my choir teacher asked us if we all remembered the first day we saw the ocean. He asked us if our first memory of the rolling waves had been imprinted in our minds, a memory so vivid and fresh that I could paint it right there and then.

The ocean attracts all people in all kinds of way. Some are afraid of it, and others love it. Either way, we all find ourselves thinking of the ocean at some points. Maybe because it's so beautiful and yet so lethal. The lost stories and men at sea are all secrets and fairytales that the ocean holds. The ocean is so powerful, that we characterize seashells as instruments that you can hear the ocean in. We listen to soundtracks of the ocean when we try to relax. The ocean is beautiful, but it has the power to drown you. And for that reason, I made the ocean a symbol of reality. When Lena says blue is forever, it means that reality is forever. You cannot escape the truth.

The reason I chose to symbolize abstract ideas through objects and colors is because it reaches another kind of understanding. You go past the definition and into a realm of experience. You create your own definition, not just something from a dictionary but something you relate to. Not something defined by words, but by emotion and personal conflict. That is the beauty, to be able to create something so raw, to make someone miss something that they never even had.

Acknowledgements

This book wouldn't be complete without the following people: my uncle, for always trying to better my writing, helping me with titles for poems, and of course for the unconditional support and articles he sends; my friends, for urging me to actually get Fallen published in the first place after reading the first draft more than three times; MICDS and our librarian, for organizing a NaNoWriMo club, because without it I would never have completed this book; my sixth grade writing teacher, for teaching me how much writing was too little and too much; my four-year-old brother, no matter how annoying he can be, for being a ball of sunshine; and most of all, thank you to my mother and father. My father, for making me smile and laugh when I'm down or tired; for being wise and leading me through my problems; for teaching me how to speak up and be brave. My mother, for comforting me in times when I needed it; for being there for me when I needed her most; for igniting the love of writing and reading in me in the first place.

Thank you.

About the Author

Haya Hussain is a 12-year-old girl in St. Louis, Missouri. She is currently a 7th grader at MICDS. She lives with her younger brother and parents. You can contact her at hussainhaya06@gmail.com.

Made in the USA
Coppell, TX
03 November 2019

10935583R00085